*For Sam and Immy x ~ B T*

*For Eddie who fills my heart with magic every day ~ A J*

LITTLE TIGER PRESS
an imprint of the Little Tiger Group
1 The Coda Centre, 189 Munster Road, London SW6 6AW
www.littletiger.co.uk
First published in Great Britain 2016
This edition published 2017

Written by Barry Timms
Text copyright © Little Tiger Press 2016, 2017
Illustrations copyright © Ag Jatkowska 2016, 2017

Ag Jatkowska has asserted her right to be identified as the illustrator
of this work under the Copyright, Designs and Patents Act, 1988

A CIP catalogue record for this book is available from the British Library
All rights reserved • ISBN 978-1-84869-682-2
Printed in China • LTP/1800/1825/0517

2 4 6 8 10 9 7 5 3 1

Barry Timms

Ag Jatkowska

# Santa to the Rescue!

LITTLE TIGER
LONDON

It was a cold Christmas Eve and the snow fell thick and deep. All through Holly Tree Forest the animals scurried, delivering their gifts and delicious treats.

"Special delivery for Badger!" called Robin.
"It must be a Christmas card," said Badger, tearing open the envelope. But inside was a letter from someone very special.
"Rabbit, Fox, come quickly!" gasped Badger. "Santa needs our help!"

Dear Badger,

The Bears of Mistletoe Mountain have been left stranded by the heavy snow. Without our help, their Christmas will be ruined! Please come at once!

Love,
Santa Claus

"We're going to meet Santa!" cheered the mice.

"Where's my woolly scarf?" fussed Hedgehog.

"Hurry!" called Badger, unfolding his map. "And bring plenty of hot cocoa!"

THUNDER FALLS

MISTLETOE MOUNTAIN

TWISTY MILL

SANTA'S GROTTO

HOLLY TREE FOREST

RIPPLE LAKE

Finally, everything was ready.

"Off we go!" they all cried, whizzing down through the trees towards Santa's grotto.

At last they arrived at Santa's home.
"I can't believe we're really here!" gasped Mole.
"My dear friends! I'm so pleased to see you!"
chuckled Santa, stepping out into the snow.
There were drinks and snacks for everyone,
and the animals soon felt warm again.

"Let's get to work," said Santa. "It's time to bring Christmas to the Bear family!"

There was much to be done and so little time.

"First we'll need gifts," said Santa, fetching their letters. "Will you help me choose?"

"Yes!" cheered the animals.

Dear Santa,

Please may I have a toy train this Christmas?

With love from Billy Bear

Dear Santa,

I'd really like a new teddy bear. Can you help?

Lots of love,
Betsy Bear
xxx

Dear Santa,
Please can I have some ice skates?

Bobby Bear x

Santa's Notebook

Next they went into the garden to make decorations.

"We'll need pinecones, holly and mistletoe," said Badger. "Mice – see what you can find."

"Let's make a wreath for the Bears' front door," cried Fox.

Soon, everyone had a job to do.

"Great work!" called Santa with a smile.

Holly sprigs
Mistletoe
Pinecones

There was one last thing to prepare – a Christmas feast.

"Let's get cooking!" cheered Hedgehog. So they whisked and baked till the kitchen was filled with the scent of spices.

"More icing!" cried Squirrel. "Hurry!"

It was nearly time to go.

"We're ready to load the sleigh," said Santa. And with a shake of the reins they were off!

High, high over the treetops they flew,
the winter moon lighting their way.
"Will we make it in time?" called Rabbit.
Santa laughed. "My reindeer
never let me down!"

With a snowy bump, they landed on Mistletoe
Mountain. The friends bustled about, clearing
snowdrifts and unpacking decorations.

Suddenly, Mr Bear rushed out. "Santa!"
he cried. "You've brought everything
we need!"

"My goodness! You've saved our
Christmas!" gasped Mrs Bear.

"That's what friends are for," chuckled Santa. "But now I must dash – there are presents still to deliver!"

They waved and cheered as Santa flew off into the snowy night.

"How kind you all are," said Mrs Bear. "Will you join us for Christmas right here on Mistletoe Mountain?"

"We'd love to!" said Badger.

"Hooray for Santa!" cried the young Bears
as they opened their special gifts.
"Three cheers for our new friends!"
called Mr Bear, raising a glass of punch.

And with music and laughter and fun for all, what a wonderful Christmas it was!

# Make **Christmas** magical with Little Tiger!

Stella J Jones · Caroline Pedler
**The Perfect Present**

**Is It Christmas Yet?**
Jane Chapman

Clement C. Moore · Mark Marshall
**The Night Before Christmas**

**When Granny SAVED Christmas**
JULIA HUBERY · CAROLINE PEDLER

**Waiting for Santa**
Steve Metzger · Alison Edgson

THE MAGICAL **SNOW GARDEN**
Tracey Corderoy · Jane Chapman

For information regarding any of the above titles or for our catalogue, please contact us:
Little Tiger Press, 1 The Coda Centre, 189 Munster Road, London SW6 6AW
Tel: 020 7385 6333 · E-mail: contact@littletiger.co.uk · www.littletiger.co.uk